May God Be
With you Always.

Lisa

Milo

Milo With A Halo

By Lisa M. Umina
Illustrated by Andrea Karcic

2003 Second Edition

© 2002 Lisa M. Umina
ISBN 0-971835-0-1-2

Submit all requests for reprints to:

Hal◯ Publishing Co.

Halo Publishing Company
P.O. Box 31844
Independence, Ohio 44131-0844
(216) 642-0861
www.halopublishing.com
Printed in China

Today, it is so important to teach children that they can openly communicate with God and have a relationship with Him. I can talk to God about anything. I am eternally grateful to my mom for instilling these values as a child and my hope is to share them with other parents.

This book is dedicated to my family.
I thank them for believing in me and encouraging me every step of the way.
I also dedicate this book to God.
Through Him all things were made possible.

– Lisa

A special dedication to Andrea Karcic's little girl,
Hailey Elizabeth Karcic-Buchenroth

God, today I am going to find my best friend.

I will ask Frank the fish.
He'll surely grant my wish.

Hello, Frank the fish. Will you be my best
friend and play with me till day's end?

"No," said Frank the fish. "You see, I'm in
water and you're out there. Without my tank
I have no air!"

I will ask Betty the bee.
She'll be my best friend, you wait and see.

Hello, Betty the bee. Will you be my best
friend and play with me till day's end?

"No," said Betty the bee. "You see, I live
in a bee's nest and have this stinger. If
you come too close, I'll sting your finger!"

I will ask Pete the pig in the mud.
He'll be my friend and I'll call him bud.

Hello, Pete the pig. Will you be my best friend
and play with me till day's end?

"No," said Pete the pig. "You see, I love my
mud and love to get dirty. You're too clean and
oh, so pretty."

I will ask Miss Bonnie Blue Jay.
She'll be my best friend today.

Hello, Miss Bonnie Blue Jay. Will you be my
best friend and play with me till day's end?

"No," said Miss Bonnie Blue Jay. "You see, I
live in a tree and you can't fly. Why don't
you give someone else a try?!"

I will go ask Freddy the frog.
He'll be fun all day long.

Hello, Freddy the frog. Will you be my best
friend and play with me till day's end?

"No," said Freddy the frog. "You see,
I live in this pond and jump on a lily.
You can't, so run along you silly."

I will ask Benny the bunny.
He's so cool and oh, so funny!

Hello, Benny the bunny. Will you be my best friend and play with me till day's end?

"No," said Benny the bunny. "You see, I love to hop very fast from danger, and I hardly know you. Yikes! A stranger!"

I will ask Copy the cat.
She'll be my friend and that'll be that.

Hello, Copy the cat. Will you be my best friend and play with me till day's end?

"No," said Copy the cat. "I'm napping on this wall. Being your friend wouldn't make sense at all."

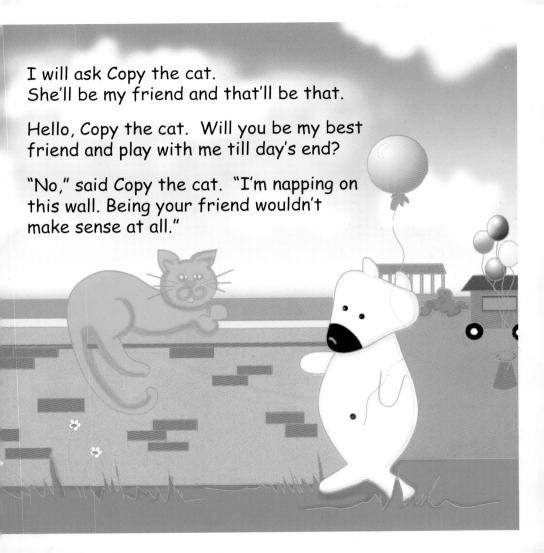

I will ask Tommy the tiger in the zoo.
He'll be my best friend, and won't tell me what to do.

Hello, Tommy the tiger. Will you be my best friend
and play with me till day's end?

"No," said Tommy the tiger. "You see, I live in the
zoo and I'm stuck in this cage. So go away before I
get in a rage!"

I will ask Andy the ant.
He'll be my friend unless he can't.

Hello, Andy the ant. Will you be my best
friend and play with me till day's end?

"No," said Andy the ant. "You see, I live in a
hill and love to crawl. You can't fit cause
you're too tall."

I will ask Mack the mole.
He's such a kind soul.

Hello, Mack the mole. Will you be my best friend and play with me till day's end?

"No," said Mack the mole. "You see, I'm down here, digging away. Why don't you come back some other day?"

I will ask Harriett the horse.
She'll be my friend, of course!

Hello, Harriett the horse. Will you be my best friend and play with me till day's end?

"No," said Harriett the horse. "I eat my hay and live in a stable. I cannot play, because I'm just not able."

"Milo...Milo, please wipe your tear and tell me what you fear."

God, I've looked high and low, all day long, to find my best friend and it all went wrong.